BOSTON BRUINS

By K.C. Kelley

THE CHILD'S WORLD®

1980 Lookout Drive • Mankato, MN 56003-1705
800-599-READ • www.childsworld.com

ACKNOWLEDGMENTS

The Child's World®: Mary Berendes, Publishing Director
Shoreline Publishing Group, LLC: James Buckley, Jr.,
   Production Director
The Design Lab: Gregory Lindholm, Design and
   Page Production

PHOTOS

Cover: AP/Wide World
Interior: AP/Wide World: 5, 6, 9, 10, 13, 17, 21, 25 top right;
   Getty Images: 18, 22, 25 left, bottom, 26, 27

LIBRARY OF CONGRESS
CATALOGING-IN-PUBLICATION DATA

Kelley, K. C.
   Boston Bruins / By K. C. Kelley.
      p. cm.
   Includes bibliographical references and index.
   ISBN 978-1-60253-438-4 (library bound : alk. paper)
   1. Boston Bruins (Hockey team)—History—Juvenile literature.
I. Title.

   GV848.B6K54 2010
   796.962'640974461—dc22

   2010015293

Printed in the United States of America
Mankato, Minnesota
September 2011
PA02108

TABLE OF CONTENTS

GO, BRUINS!

The air is chilly, but the action is heating up. The Boston Bruins race down the ice. Suddenly, a Bruin blasts the **puck** toward the net. It zooms past the **goalie** and into the net for a goal! Bruins win! Boston fans jump out of their seats and scream with excitement . . . it's another victory! Let's meet the Boston Bruins.

5

Mark Recchi and Patrice Bergeron celebrate another goal for the Boston Bruins!

In a Northeast Division game, a crowd of Bruins and Senators await a shot from a Senators player.

WHO ARE THE BOSTON BRUINS?

The Boston Bruins play in the National Hockey League (NHL). They are one of 30 teams in the NHL. The NHL includes the Eastern Conference and the Western Conference. The Bruins play in the Northeast Division of the Eastern Conference. The playoffs end with the winners of the Eastern and Western conferences facing off. The champion wins the **Stanley Cup**. The Bruins have won five Stanley Cups.

WHERE THEY CAME FROM

The Bruins first hit the ice in 1924. They were the first team from the United States in the NHL. Before 1924, all the teams in the NHL played in Canada. (Today, there are still six NHL teams in Canada.) The Bruins were also one of the Original Six—the first teams in the NHL. The Bruins won their first Stanley Cup in 1929. Many players in the **Hockey Hall of Fame** wore the black-and-gold Bruins colors. Boston's greatest years came in the early 1970s. That's when they were lead by superstar **defenseman** Bobby Orr.

Eddie Shore was the first great Bruins player. He helped the team win the NHL title in 1929.

In 2010, the Bruins played a special outdoor game against the Philadelphia Flyers at Fenway Park. That's usually the home of baseball's Red Sox!

WHO THEY PLAY

The Boston Bruins play 82 games each season. They play all the other teams in their division six times. The other Northeast Division teams are the Buffalo Sabres, the Ottawa Senators, the Montreal Canadiens, and the Toronto Maple Leafs. The Bruins and the Canadiens are fierce **rivals**. The Bruins also play other teams in the Eastern and Western Conferences.

WHERE THEY PLAY

The Bruins play their home games in an **arena** called TD Garden. Before 2005, the Bruins played in the legendary Boston Garden. They played in that smaller arena from 1928 to 1995. It was one of hockey's most-loved rinks because of its great sports history. Fans watched the Bruins win five NHL championships and enjoyed thousands of amazing moments in the Boston Garden.

The Bruins stretch before a game at the TD Garden. The team's famous "B" logo is painted under the ice.

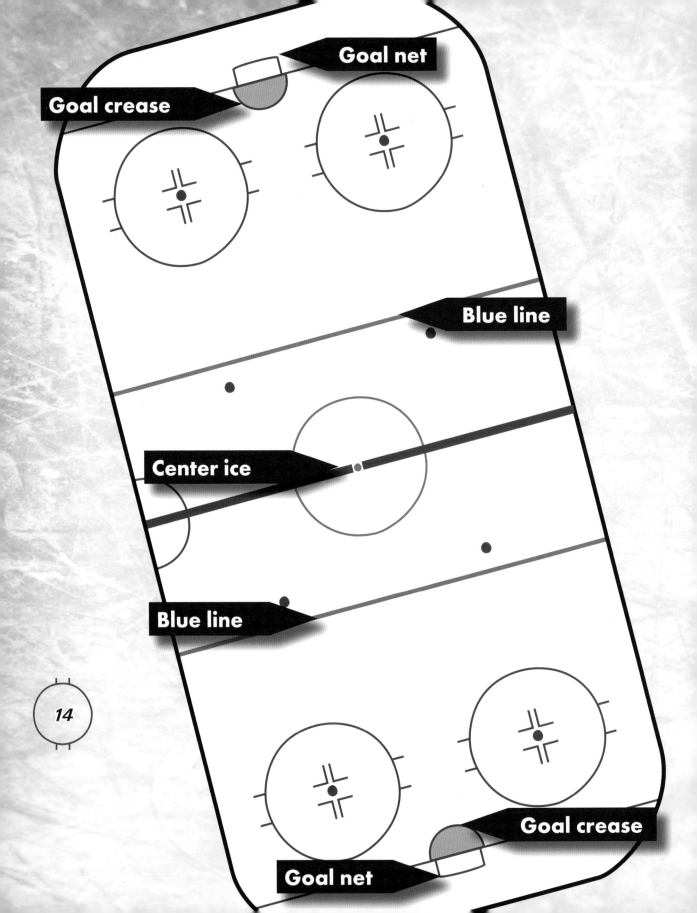

Goal net

Goal crease

Blue line

Center ice

Blue line

14

Goal crease

Goal net

THE HOCKEY RINK

Hockey games are played on a sheet of ice called a rink. It is a rounded rectangle. NHL rinks are 200 feet (61 m) long and 85 feet (26 m) wide. Wooden boards surround the entire rink. Clear plastic panels are on top of the boards so fans can see the action and be protected from flying pucks. Netting is hung above the seats at each end of the rink to catch any wild pucks. The goal nets are near each end of the rink. Each net is four feet (1.2 m) high and six feet (1.8 m) wide. A red line marks the center of the ice. Blue lines mark each team's defensive zone.

THE PUCK

An NHL puck is made of very hard rubber. The disk is three inches (76 mm) wide and 1 inch (25 mm) thick. It weighs about 6 ounces (170 g). It's black so it's easy to see on the ice. Many pucks are used during a game, because some fly into the stands.

BIG DAYS!

The Bruins have had many great seasons in their long history. Here are three of the greatest:

1928–29: Led by Eddie Shore, the Bruins won their first Stanley Cup championship.

1940–41: The Bruins won a record 23 straight games to finish the season in first place. They went on to win their third Stanley Cup.

1969–70: The Bruins won their first Stanley Cup in 30 seasons. A famous photo showed Bobby Orr flying through the air as he scored the winning goal.

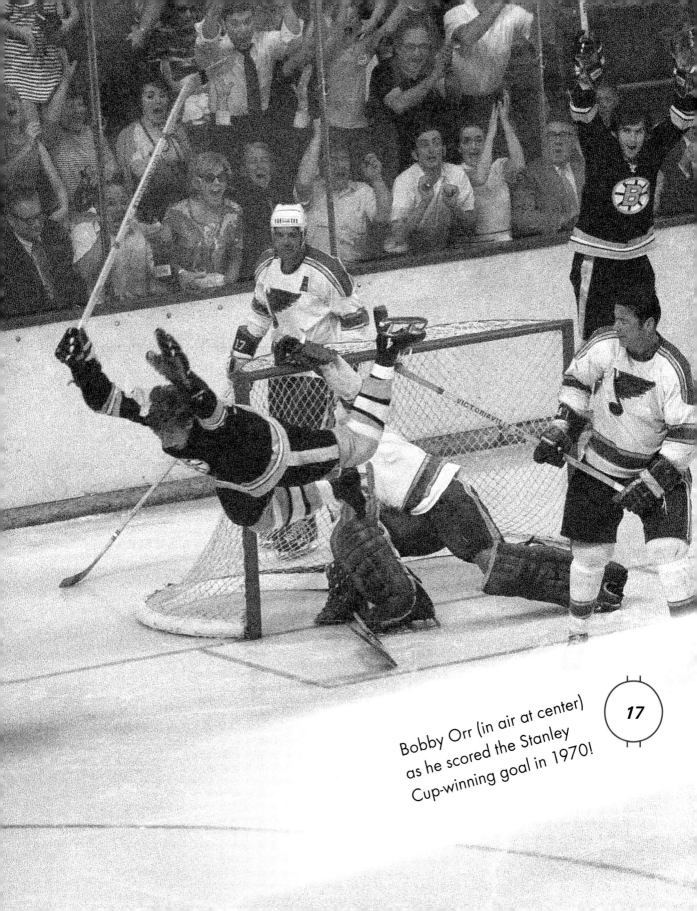

Bobby Orr (in air at center) as he scored the Stanley Cup-winning goal in 1970!

Rookie goalie Robbie Tallas couldn't stop this 1997 shot . . . and the Bruins lost again!

TOUGH DAYS!

Not every season can end with a Stanley Cup championship. Here are some of the toughest seasons in Bruins' history.

1924–25: The Bruins had a slow start. They won only six games in their first season!

1989–90: A great season ended sadly. After leading the NHL with 101 **points**, the Bruins lost in the Stanley Cup finals to the Edmonton Oilers.

1996–97: The Bruins missed the playoffs for the first time since 1967. The team had the fewest points in the NHL.

MEET THE FANS

Boston Bruins fans love their team! They pack TD Garden to cheer for the Bruins. The team's home is in Boston. But hockey-loving fans all over New England also root for the Bruins. New England has cold winters, and hockey is a very popular sport to watch and play there. Families have cheered and played together for decades. Many fans have a short nickname for the team: the Bs.

BRIDGE[...] NHL Winter CLASSIC [...]COM

THOMAS
30

21

Bruins fans cheered goalie Tim Thomas during the 2010 outdoor game at Fenway Park.

Bobby Orr was the most famous player in Bruins history.

HEROES THEN...

The Bruins have had dozens of star players. Here are just a few. Defenseman Eddie Shore won four Most Valuable Player (MVP) awards and helped Boston win the 1929 Stanley Cup. Left **wing** John "Chief" Bucyk was a scoring machine. He's still the team's all-time leader in goals. Phil Esposito was another great goal-scorer. "Espo" led the NHL in goals six times from his **center** position. Bobby Orr is called the greatest defenseman ever. He set many records and helped the Bruins win two Stanley Cups. Ray Bourque was another great defenseman. He was a Bruin for 20 seasons. Right wing Cam Neely's great career led him to the Hockey Hall of Fame.

HEROES NOW...

The Bruins boast some of the top players in the NHL. Bruins **captain** Zdeno Chara from Slovakia was named the NHL's top defenseman in 2009. He has the hardest shot in the NHL—105.4 mph (169.6 kph)! Body-slamming left wing Milan Lucic is one of the league's toughest players. **Veteran** Mark Recchi has more points than any other active NHL player. He gives the team great leadership, too. Patrice Bergeron is another top scorer for the Bs. In the net for Boston is Tim Thomas. The Michigan native won the 2009 Vezina Trophy as the NHL's top goalie. He played for the United States in the 2010 Winter Olympics, too.

DEFENSEMAN

ZDENO CHARA

LEFT WING

MILAN LUCIC

GOALIE

TIM THOMAS

25

GEARING UP

Hockey players wear short pants and a jersey called a "sweater." Underneath, they wear lots of pads to protect themselves. They also wear padded gloves and a hard plastic helmet. They wear special ice hockey skates with razor-sharp blades. They carry a stick to handle the puck.

Goalies wear special gloves to help them block and catch shots. They have extra padding on their legs, chest, and arms. They also wear special decorated helmets and use a larger stick.

26

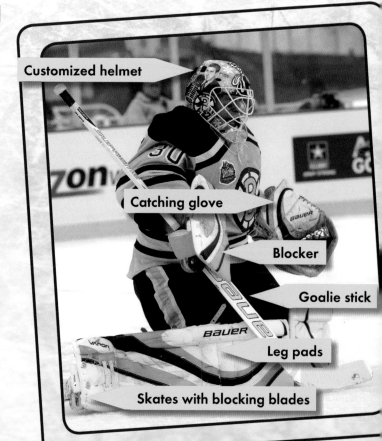

Customized helmet

Catching glove

Blocker

Goalie stick

Leg pads

Skates with blocking blades

Helmet

Face shield

Shoulder pads

Sweater

Gloves

Knee pads

Stick

Shin guards

27

Skates

SPORTS STATS

Here are some all-time career records for the Boston Bruins.
All the stats are through the 2009–2010 season.

HOT SHOTS

GOALS

These players have scored the most career goals for the Bruins.

PLAYER	GOALS
John Bucyk	545
Phil Esposito	459

PERFECT PASSERS

ASSISTS

These players have the most career assists on the team.

PLAYER	ASSISTS
Raymond Bourque	1,111
John Bucyk	794

BIG SCORES!

POINTS

These players have the most points, a combination of goals and assists.

PLAYER	POINTS
Raymond Bourque	1,506
John Bucyk	1,339

SUPER SAVERS

GOALS AGAINST AVERAGE

These Boston goalies have allowed the fewest goals per game in their career.

PLAYER	GAA
Tiny Thompson	1.99
Byron Dafoe	2.30

PLAYER POSITIVE

CAREER PLUS-MINUS

These players have the best **plus-minus** in Bruins history.

PLAYER	PLUS-MINUS
Bobby Orr	+589
Raymond Bourque	+494

FROM THE BENCH

COACHES

These coaches have the most wins in Bruins history.

COACH	WINS
Art Ross	361
Milt Schmidt	245

29

GLOSSARY

arena an indoor place for sports

assist a play that gives the puck to the player who scores a goal

captain a player chosen to lead his team on and off the ice

center a hockey position at the middle of the forward, offensive line

defenseman a player who takes a position closest to his own goal, to keep the puck out

goalie the goaltender, whose job is to keep pucks out of the net

Hockey Hall of Fame located in Toronto, Ontario, this museum honors the greatest players in the sport's history

plus-minus a player gets a plus one for being on the ice when their team scores a goal, and a minus one when the other team scores a goal; the total of these pluses and minuses creates this stat. The better players always have high plus ratings

points a team gets two points for every game they win and one point for every game they tie; a player gets a point for every goal he scores and another point for every assist

puck the hard, frozen rubber disk used when playing hockey

rivals teams that play each other often and with great intensity

rookie a player in his first season in a pro league

Stanley Cup the trophy awarded each year to the winner of the National Hockey League championship

veteran an athlete who has been a pro for many years

wing a hockey position on the outside left or right of the forward line

FIND OUT MORE

BOOKS

Leonetti, Michael. *Number Four, Bobby Orr*. Vancouver: Raincoast Books, 2003.

Nichols, John. *Boston Bruins: NHL History & Heroes*. Toronto: Saunders Book Co., 2009.

Thomas, Kelly, and John Kicksee. *Inside Hockey!: The Legends, Facts, and Feats that Made the Game*. Toronto: Maple Leaf Press, 2008.

WEB SITES

Visit our Web page for links about the Boston Bruins and other pro hockey teams.

childsworld.com/links

Note to Parents, Teachers, and Librarians: We routinely verify our Web links to make sure they are safe, active sites—so encourage your readers to check them out!

31

INDEX

ABOUT THE AUTHOR

K.C. Kelley has written dozens of books on sports for young readers. He has also been a youth baseball and soccer coach. When he was a kid, he spent a lot of time rooting for the Los Angeles Kings and playing street hockey.